Mary Bertha McKenzie Toland

Atlina

Queen of the Floating Isle

Mary Bertha McKenzie Toland

Atlina
Queen of the Floating Isle

ISBN/EAN: 9783743418547

Manufactured in Europe, USA, Canada, Australia, Japa

Cover: Foto ©Andreas Hilbeck / pixelio.de

Manufactured and distributed by brebook publishing software
(www.brebook.com)

Mary Bertha McKenzie Toland

Atlina

ATLINA

M.B.M. TOLAND

ATLINA

QVEEN·OF·THE·FLOATING·

ISLE

BY

M.B.M.TOLAND

J.B.LIPPINCOTT Co.
MDCCCXCIII.

PRINTED BY J. B. LIPPINCOTT COMPANY, PHILADELPHIA.

THIS VOLUME IS GRATEFULLY
DEDICATED TO THE ARTISTS
DRAWINGS HAVE EMBELLISHED
MY WORKS

M. ROBERTS

LIST OF DRAWINGS

Ornamental title-page, frontispiece, half-titles to the Cantos, and decorative designs throughout the text,

Artist, A. F. JACCACI.

CANTO I

Ages ago, Atlantis proudly swayed

   Her prehistoric glories, unsurpassed;

The God Posei'don, regally arrayed,

   With trident sceptre, mystic marvels cast

O'er that strange continent.

                    His power supreme

Enriched the earth with wondrous splendors grand,

   Enthroned to rule and realize the dream

Of fabled mysteries o'er sea and land.

   So reigned this Neptune king with will profound

As o'er a world.

                Virtues he there enshrined

With wisdom, justice, truth, and laws renowned

   That good-will meted unto all mankind.

Transcendent beauties brightly beamed upon
　　The fertile plain, fairest of all the world;
Near which a mount uprose above the lawn,
　　Where stately palms and tropic plants unfurled
'Neath sunshine flooding its life-giving rays
　　O'er budding blossoms, blooming everywhere.
There fountains jetted iridescent sprays
　　Near groves of stately trees,—exotics rare;
While streams meandered and fresh bubbling springs
　　Of purest waters fertilized the sod,
And breathing zephyrs wafted as with wings
　　Sweet, odorous incense offered to their God.

Upon this mount dwelt one primeval pair.

Their only child, a daughter scarcely grown,

In dawning womanhood was wondrous fair.

When her fond parents died, leaving alone

This lovely orphan (Cleito was her name),

Poseidon met her, pleased with her pure grace.

He elevated to exalted fame

One made by nature worthy of that place.

His heart idealized this mortal love.

Around her palace he alternately

Drew two encircling zones,—of land above,—

Grand terraces. Three smaller zones of sea

Enclosed the citadel of destiny.

No man could enter that enchanted spot,—

   Himself a god, his wishes naught could mar;

All rarest treasures to the isle he brought

   That beamed in beauty like a brilliant star;

For in the rocks all precious gems were found;

   With purest gold and silver, veins of ore

There threaded through. The mount, within, around,

   With richest offerings that nature bore.

Three walls enclosed the isle;

               An outer wall

Coated with brass; the next with tin o'erlaid;

   The next of ori'chalch; glowing through all

Red lights that blazed warm flashes as they played.

V.

'Tween citadel and palace stately stood

A holy temple, in the centre, where

Poseidon with his Cleito blessings wooed

In bliss divine, the joys of life to share;

Each year fruit-offerings by them were brought

From ten divisions of that wondrous isle

As sacred sacrifice.

On hallowed spot

Poseidon's own fane stood in grandest style,—

Barbaric splendor, stadium in length

With half a stadium in width.

Its height

Proportionate, throughout of massive strength,

Aglow with brilliant gems emitting light.

This edifice in silver was encased,

    With pinnacles bestudded, gleaming gold:

An ivory roof within, its borders graced

    By royal decorations, sunbeam stoled.

Shimmered forth from the pillars, walls, and floor

    Bedazzling rays of every precious gem

That flashed with glowing lights the arches o'er.

    Poseidon's statue, crowned with diadem,

In regal robes upon his chariot stood,

    With six winged horses, thus in state to guide

His flying steed.

        Ruler divine, endued

With power supreme o'er all things to preside.

One hundred Nereids on dolphins rode

    As if ambassadors from the deep sea;

Colossal golden statues brightly glowed

    Around the altar of their deity;

Engraved on columned orichalch that stood

    Within the temple, holy laws were given

To teach the right, commanding all things good

    Through virtue's path, to make this world like heaven.

Outside the temple rose ten golden kings,

    Ten golden statues of their wives in state,

With many tributes, sacred offerings,

    Impressive rites whence glories radiate.

VIII.

Thus many generations passed away

   Since God Poseidon's first-born reigned as king.

His wise descendants aided the display

   Of peerless pageantry the years could bring.

Supremacy to Atlas' line was shown,

   With binding rule on all the kings impressed;

No wars to join against each other's throne,

   But render aid, if enemies oppressed;

Vast multitudes inhabited the land,

   Thousands of chariots for war arrayed.

Twelve hundred ships awaited their command,

   With officers and honors grand displayed.

While god-like nature lasted in that race

  To laws divine obedience was given,

With true devotion to their gods in grace

  As children taught inheritance of heaven;

The Gold and Silver Ages having passed,

  Then Bronze Age followed, scattering the seed

Of discord, avarice, with sins o'ercast,

  Admixture more of human, selfish greed.

Lost were the virtues of Poseidon's reign,

  Then Zeus, the God of gods, with will supreme,

Called all the gods, his mandate to make plain,

  To judge with justice, and lost rights redeem.

No archives chronicle the God's decree
   That doomed Atlantis to its sudden fate.
By tempest torn and sunk beneath the sea,
   Their mortal sins to thus obliterate ;
One portion of the land eruptions cleft
   Just as it stood, with sacred temples, throne,
And royal palace, all that had been left
   Of grandest continent the world had known.
A pious family protected, saved
   With their attendants faithful cast away,
On this wrecked isle the many dangers braved
   By guardian care, on that eventful day.

II.

While these were offering orisons that morn,

   Fierce, warring elements in fury hurled

The earth, that lifted, trembled, then was torn

   Asunder from that cursed and sinking world.

Prostrate before the altar they remained,

   Until was heard a voice from one unseen,

"Thy godliness and virtues pure have gained

   Pardon for thee and thine.   As shall be seen

From guardian care, all good will emulate,

   This holy isle for thee is saved and blessed,

Thy heirs shall reign as kings, and reinstate

   Poseidon's line, as God Zeus thinketh best."

III

This godly family had one fair child,

    A daughter, beaming love and fond delight

And wondrous beauty as she sweetly smiled,

    While shimmered o'er her brow soft halos bright,

Through airy tresses, like warm rays of gold,

    That flowed in careless waves around her form.

Her large blue eyes would evening's shade enfold,

    Her cheeks, the sea-shell's tint, with blushes warm.

No fairer mortal maiden ere was seen ;

    Her charms of manner bore a winsome way.

Crowned was she on the Floating Isle as queen

    O'er sea and land in glorious array.

IV.

Her palace pearled with golden settings rare,

   Its temples blending treasures of all climes :

Her bowers were draped with climbing flowers fair

   O'er gleaming domes that measured music's chimes ;

Her Nereid attendants served with love ;

   They hovered near the Floating Isle with pride

On dolphins, their devotion thus to prove,

   Played timbrels, dancing on the rippling tide ;

Her parents in their temple offered praise,

   Gave thanks to Zeus with offerings and prayer ;

They taught Atlina's life pure, holy ways

   To thus repay the gods for guardian care.

Atlina just attained her womanhood,

  With voice like angel's voice, soft, low, and sweet ;

And speaking glances.

              Thoughts were understood

Ere spoken, if the listener chanced to meet

  Their trusting light from soul of purity.

Last heiress of lost kings was she, this isle,

  Her only heritage, World of the Sea.

That meted glorious destiny!   Meanwhile

  Her subjects wished their lovely queen to wed

A god-like king.   They made their wishes known,

  And often to the subject pleading led

That heirs of Atlas' line might grace her throne.

With joy the Nereids appeared one morn

   Arrayed in mantles of fair sprays of mist,

Their ruddy shoulders lightly to adorn.

   Atlina's hand devotedly they kissed,

And signalled galleys, coming near the shore

   Upon the ocean's brightly beaming breast

So near the isle, a voice in clear command

   Cried, "Lower sails!

                  Drop anchor!   Here we rest!

This is the world we've sought so long in vain.

   How wondrous beautiful, this heavenly sphere,

Deus has our labors blessed!

                  'Tis glory's gain ;

   This blissful haven offers royal cheer."

VII

Enthroned in regal state the youthful queen

  Awaited the approach of strangers grand,

Enrobed most gorgeously, as if to wean

  Her thoughts from all except a queen's command :

Yet flitting blushes warmed the cold repose

  Of stately dignity. Her scarf confined

By opal stars, their tints like fair rainbows

  That shimmered halos, happiness enshrined ;

As come the heralds, with their god-like king,

  He knelt before her, conquered.

                    Beauty's power

Enhanced the scene. The sprites were welcoming

  With timbrel shells and song, that happy hour.

SONG.

I.

Ripple,

Dipple!

Sever

Waves with rhapsody!

Lightly,

Sprightly

Ever,

Laugh in gladsome glee!

II.

Meeting,

Greeting,

Meekly,

Heroes of the Deep!

Suing,

Wooing

Sweetly,

Joys within their keep.

III.

Waving,

Laving,

Brightly,

Kindest welcome bring.

Proving,

Loving,

Rightly,

Welcome to our king.

VIII

Atlina listened with a pleased surprise

    To courtly compliments, profusely paid,

Awaking glances, beamed from dreamy eyes,

    O'er dimpling smiles where flitting blushes played;

While spake Diotheus fond words of praise:

    He thanked the gods who his adventures blessed,

That from a sinking world the isle released,

    And guided him to this fair land of rest

To realize a love, his heart to feast:

    " My ships lie waiting for my precious prize

To bear in triumph to my favored throne,

    My kingdom waits, where dips the eastern skies,

A goddess queen, for every virtue known."

IX

At once she sought the temple to confide

   Her new found happiness.

                   With fond caress

She coyly knelt her father's knee beside,

   With warmest blushes new life to confess;

He answered rising, with uplifted hand:

   "Obedience is due the gods' decree!

Thy duty, child, must follow their command,

   Their sacred will thus metes thy destiny."

The mother's arms enclasped her daughter's waist,

   "Child of our love! thanks to the gods divine

Who taught thee love with true devotion graced,

   Our happiness reflects this joy of thine."

CANTO III

ALL nature beamed with beauties unsurpassed,

The sun in glory showered dazzling rays

And banished shadows ; not a cloud o'ercast

That nuptial morn, hailed with exalted praise.

Awaking zephyrs trilled a flitting breeze ;

Sweet carols sang wild birds in gladsome glee ;

Æolians were sighing through the trees

With joy and sadness, varied melody.

The Floating Isle, nestled its border bowers

Of tropic plants, wafting perfumes full sweet,

From countless cups of all its precious flowers

Which incense offered, odorous, replete.

Directed by the gods, Diotheus left

    Aurosa Greece (his kingdom)—journeyed o'er

The inland seas, seeking that portion cleft

    From doomed Atlantis.

                Near southwestern shore

Of broad Atlantic main, he found the isle,

    Its goddess queen, to grace his Grecian throne,

Won by her loveliness. Sweet was her smile

    With happiness, to him before unknown.

Adina donned the graceful Grecian gown,

    Pure as the pearling dew born of the air:

Her every wish with joy the king to crown,

    Through life his love to keep and ever share.

III.

Lifted were anchors, sails unfurled, outspread,
　　The fleet unmoored, ready to sail away.
When fond attendants stately measures led:
　　An invocation to the God of day.

Thou God! The sun!
　　O light of light!
Thou glorious one!
　　O radiance bright,
　　　Divine!
Guard with thy care
　　With wisdom, might,
Our queen, to share
　　What seemeth right
　　　As thine.

O glorious Sun!
  From care released,
Their voyage when done
  May joyous feast
    Extend!
Welcome with bliss!
  In the far east,
Sweeter than this,
  All pleasures feast
    And bend.

IV.

Atlina with Diotheus reclined

    'Neath gleaming canopy of threaded gold,

Begemmed with crest of double crowns, entwined

    That fond predictions for their future told.

The god-like king, of stately presence grand,

    His massive brow alight with new-found bliss,

Was hero of victorious command ;

    But conquered worlds could not compare with this.

His classic features, perfectly were lined ;

    His earnest eyes of evening's darkest shade,

His beard and raven locks flowed, waved, entwined

    And shimmered raven lights, where sunbeams

        strayed.

V.

Then floated banners, with a loud acclaim
  Of oarsmen measuring each deep-drawn stroke,
While tearful voices sighed Atlina's name
  Amid the pageantry, farewells awoke.
Thus glided they o'er ocean's throbbing breast,
  The groom and bride guarded from every ill.
When Floating Isle receded on the west,
  Atlina's heart was pained with saddened thrill:
Diotheus fond words repressed to wean
  Her heart from yearning thoughts with better cheer:
Such silent sympathy impressed his queen
  With warmer gratitude to one most dear.

VI.

While lingering rays, reflected from sunbeams,

    Bedecked the ocean's slowly-throbbing breast.

Its waves aglow, were rippling brightest gleams,

    Ere evening shadows wooed the day to rest.

In mantled mist, the scenes dissolved away

    With angel voices chantant on the air;

The mighty deep intoned its plashing spray,

    While guardian dolphins hovered near with care.

The nautilus its stately measures bore

    Like royal page—and glided gracefully

Beside the galleys, dipped the waters o'er

    In unison with songs of air and sea.

VII

The day was blushing, as approaching night
   Unfurled its glowing colors in the west,
When lo! a mirage, framed with ruby light,
   Of Floating Isle in tropic beauties dressed
Above the low horizon lifted there,
   With halos, lingering rays of setting sun:
Its sacred temples pictured in air
   That mystic hour when day its course hath run.
"See!" cried Diotheus, "my dreams unfold;
   This scene the gods predicted unto me:
'Thou shalt Atlina's Floating Isle behold
   Uplifted to the skies, 'tis God's decree.'"

www.ingramcontent.com/pod-product-compliance
Lightning Source LLC
Chambersburg PA
CBHW030026030726
47499CB00008B/3131